THE YATES PRIDE

A Romance

MORE WILDSIDE CLASSICS

THE YATES PRIDE
A Romance

MARY E.
WILKINS FREEMAN

WILDSIDE PRESS

THE YATES PRIDE

This edition published 2005 by Wildside Press, LLC.
www.wildsidepress.com

PART I

♦

Opposite Miss Eudora Yates's old colonial mansion was the perky modern Queen Anne residence of Mrs. Joseph Glynn. Mrs. Glynn had a daughter, Ethel, and an unmarried sister, Miss Julia Esterbrook. All three were fond of talking, and had many callers who liked to hear the feebly effervescent news of Wellwood. This afternoon three ladies were there: Miss Abby Simson, Mrs. John Bates, and Mrs. Edward Lee. They sat in the Glynn sitting-room, which shrilled with treble voices as if a flock of sparrows had settled therein.

The Glynn sitting-room was charming, mainly because of the quantity of flowering plants. Every window was filled with them, until the room seemed like a conservatory. Ivy, too, climbed over the pictures, and the mantel-shelf was a cascade of wandering Jew, growing in old china vases.

"Your plants are really wonderful, Mrs. Glynn," said Mrs. Bates, "but I don't see how you manage to get a glimpse of anything outside the house, your windows are so full of them."

"Maybe she can see and not be seen," said Abby Simson, who had a quick wit and a ready tongue.

Mrs. Joseph Glynn flushed a little. "I have not the slightest curiosity about my neighbors," she said, "but it is impossible to live just across the road from any house without knowing something of what is going on, whether one looks or not," said she, with dignity.

"Ma and I never look out of the windows from curiosity," said Ethel Glynn, with spirit. Ethel Glynn had a great deal of spirit, which was evinced in her personal appearance as well as her tongue. She had an eye to the fashions; her sleeves were never out of date, nor was the arrangement of her hair.

"For instance," said Ethel, "we never look at the house opposite because we are at all prying, but we do know that that old maid has been doing a mighty queer thing lately."

"First thing you know you will be an old maid yourself, and then your stones will break your own glass house," said Abby Simson.

"Oh, I don't care," retorted Ethel. "Nowadays an old maid isn't an old maid except from choice, and everybody knows it. But it must have been different in Miss Eudora's time. Why, she is older than you are, Miss Abby."

"Just five years," replied Abby, unruffled, "and she had chances, and I know it."

"Why didn't she take them, then?"

"Maybe," said Abby, "girls had choice then as much as now, but I never could make out why she didn't marry Harry Lawton."

Ethel gave her head a toss. "Maybe," said she, "once in a while, even so long ago, a girl wasn't so crazy to get married as folks thought. Maybe she didn't want him."

"She did want him," said Abby. "A girl doesn't get so pale and peaked-looking for nothing as Eudora Yates did, after she had dismissed Harry Lawton and he had gone away, nor haunt the post-office as she used to, and, when she didn't get a letter, go away looking as if she would die."

"Maybe," said Ethel, "her folks were opposed."

"Nobody ever opposed Eudora Yates except her own self," replied Abby. "Her father was dead, and Eudora's ma thought the sun rose and set in her. She would never have opposed her if she had wanted to marry a foreign duke or the old Harry himself."

"I remember it perfectly," said Mrs. Joseph Glynn.

"So do I," said Julia Esterbrook.

"Don't see why you shouldn't. You were plenty old enough to have your memory in good working order if it was ever going to be," said Abby Simson.

"Well," said Ethel, "it is the funniest thing I ever heard of. If a girl wanted a man enough to go all to pieces over him, and he wanted her, why on earth didn't she take him?"

"Maybe they quarreled," ventured Mrs. Edward Lee, who was a mild, sickly-looking woman and seldom expressed an opinion.

"Well, that might have been," agreed Abby, "although Eudora always had the name of having a beautiful disposition."

"I have always found," said Mrs. Joseph Glynn, with an air of wisdom, "that it is the beautiful dispositions which are the most set the minute they get a start the wrong way. It is the always-flying-out people who are the easiest to get on with in the long run."

"Well," said Abby, "maybe that is so, but folks might get worn all to a frazzle by the flying-out ones before the long run. I'd rather take my chances with a woman like Eudora. She always seems just so, just as calm and sweet. When the Ames's barn, that was next to hers, burned down and the wind was her way, she just walked in and out of her house, carrying the things she valued most, and she looked like a picture — somehow she had got all dressed fit to make calls — and there wasn't a muscle of her face that seemed to move. Eudora Yates is to my mind the most beautiful woman in this town, old or young, I don't care who she is."

"I suppose," said Julia Esterbrook, "that she has a lot of money."

"I wonder if she has," said Mrs. John Bates.

The others stared at her. "What makes you think she hasn't?" Mrs. Glynn inquired, sharply.

"Nothing," said Mrs. Bates, and closed her thin lips. She would say no more, but the others had suspicions, because her husband, John Bates, was a wealthy business man.

"I can't believe she has lost her money," said Mrs. Glynn. "She wouldn't have been such a fool as to do what she has if she hadn't money."

"What has she done?" asked Mrs. Bates, eagerly.

"What has she done?" asked Abby, and Mrs. Lee looked up inquiringly.

The faces of Mrs. Glynn, her daughter, and her

sister became important, full of sly and triumphant knowledge.

"Haven't you heard?" asked Mrs. Glynn.

"Yes, haven't you?" asked Ethel.

"Haven't any of you heard?" asked Julia Esterbrook.

"No," admitted Abby, rather feebly. "I don't know as I have."

"Do you mean about Eudora's going so often to the Lancaster girls' to tea?" asked Mrs. John Bates, with a slight bridle of possible knowledge.

"I heard of that," said Mrs. Lee, not to be outdone.

"Land, no," replied Mrs. Glynn. "Didn't she always go there? It isn't that. It is the most unheard-of thing she had done; but no woman, unless she had plenty of money to bring it up, would have done it."

"To bring what up?" asked Abby, sharply. Her eyes looked as small and bright as needles.

Julia regarded her with intense satisfaction. "What do women generally bring up?" said she.

"I don't know of anything they bring up, whether they have it or not, except a baby," retorted Abby, sharply.

Julia wilted a little; but her sister, Mrs. Glynn, was not perturbed. She launched her thunderbolt of news at once, aware that the critical moment had come, when the quarry of suspicion had left the bushes.

"She has adopted a baby," said she, and paused like a woman who had fired a gun, half scared herself and shrinking from the report.

Ethel seconded her mother. "Yes," said she, "Miss

Eudora has adopted a baby, and she has a baby-carriage, and she wheels it out any time she takes a notion." Ethel's speech was of the nature of an after-climax. The baby-carriage weakened the situation.

The other women seized upon the idea of the carriage to cover their surprise and prevent too much gloating on the part of Mrs. Glynn, Ethel, and Julia.

"Is it a new carriage?" inquired Mrs. Lee.

"No, it looks like one that came over in the ark," retorted Mrs. Glynn. Then she repeated: "She has adopted a baby," but this time there was no effect of an explosion. However, the treble chorus rose high, "Where did she get the baby? Was it a boy or a girl? Why did she adopt it? Did it cry much?" and other queries, none of which Mrs. Glynn, Ethel, and Julia could answer very decidedly except the last. They all announced that the adopted baby was never heard to cry at all.

"Must be a very good child," said Abby.

"Must be a very healthy child," said Mrs. Lee, who had had experience with crying babies.

"Well, she has it, anyhow," said Mrs. Glynn.

Right upon the announcement came proof. The beautiful door of the old colonial mansion opposite was thrown open, and clumsy and cautious motion was evident. Presently a tall, slender woman came down the path between the box borders, pushing a baby-carriage. It was undoubtedly a very old carriage. It must have dated back to the fifties, if not the forties. It was made of wood, with a leather buggy-top, and was evidently very heavy.

Abby eyed it shrewdly. "If I am not mistaken," said she, "that is the very carriage Eudora herself was wheeled around in when she was a baby. I am almost sure I have seen that identical carriage before. When we were girls I used to go to the Yates house sometimes. Of course, it was always very formal, a little tea-party for Eudora, with her mother on hand, but I feel sure that I saw that carriage there one of those times.

"I suppose it cost a lot of money, in the time of it. The Yateses always got the very best for Eudora," said Julia. "And maybe Eudora goes about so little she doesn't realize how out of date the carriage is, but I should think it would be very heavy to wheel, especially if the baby is a good-sized one."

"It looks like a very large baby," said Ethel. "Of course, it is so rolled up we can't tell."

"Haven't you gone out and asked to see the baby?" said Abby.

"Would we dare unless Eudora Yates offered to show it?" said Julia, with a surprised air; and the others nodded assent. Then they all crowded to the front windows and watched from behind the screens of green flowering things. It was very early in the spring. Fairly hot days alternated with light frosts. The trees were touched with sprays of rose and gold and gold-green, but the wind still blew cold from the northern snows, and the occupant of Eudora's ancient carriage was presumably wrapped well to shelter it from harm. There was, in fact, nothing to be seen in the carriage, except a large roll of blue and white, as Eudora emerged from the yard and closed the iron gate of the tall fence behind her.

Through this fence pricked the evergreen box, and the deep yard was full of soft pastel tints of reluctantly budding trees and bushes. There was one deep splash of color from a yellow bush in full bloom.

Eudora paced down the sidewalk with a magnificent, stately gait. There was something rather magnificent in her whole appearance. Her skirts of old, but rich, black fabric swept about her long, advancing limbs; she held her black-bonneted head high, as if crowned. She pushed the cumbersome baby-carriage with no apparent effort. An ancient India shawl was draped about her sloping shoulders.

Eudora, as she passed the Glynn house, turned her face slightly, so that its pure oval was evident. She was now a beauty in late middle life. Her hair, of an indeterminate shade, swept in soft shadows over her ears; her features were regular; her expression was at once regal and gentle. A charm which was neither of youth nor of age reigned in her face; her grace had surmounted with triumphant ease the slope of every year. Eudora passed out of sight with the baby-carriage, lifting her proud lady-head under the soft droop of the spring boughs; and her inspectors, whom she had not seen, moved back from the Glynn windows with exclamations of astonishment.

"I wonder," said Abby, "whether she will have that baby call her ma or aunty."

Meantime Eudora passed down the village street until she reached the Lancaster house, about half a mile away on the same side. There dwelt the Misses Amelia and Anna Lancaster, who were about Eudora's age, and a widowed sister, Mrs. Sophia Willing, who was much older. The Lancaster house was also a colonial mansion, much after the fashion of Eudora's, but it showed signs of continued opulence. Eudora's, behind her trees and leafing vines, was gray for lack of paint. Some of the colonial ornamental details about porches and roof were sloughing off or had already disappeared. The Lancaster house gleamed behind its grove of evergreen trees as white and perfect as in its youth. The windows showed rich slants of draperies behind their green glister of old glass.

A gardener, with a boy assistant, was at work in the grounds when Eudora entered. He touched his cap. He was an old man who had lived with the Lancasters ever since Eudora could remember. He advanced toward her now. "Sha'n't Tommy push — the baby-carriage up to the house for you, Miss Eudora?" he said, in his cracked old voice.

Eudora flushed slightly, and, as if in response, the old man flushed, also. "No, I thank you, Wilson," she said, and moved on.

The boy, who was raking dry leaves, stood gazing at them with a shrewd, whimsical expression. He was the old man's grandson.

"Is that a boy or a girl kid, grandpa?" he inquired, when the gardener returned.

"Hold your tongue!" replied the old man, irascibly. Suddenly he seized the boy by his two thin little shoulders with knotted old hands.

"Look at here, Tommy, whatever you know, you keep your mouth shet, and whatever you don't know, you keep your mouth shet, if you know what's good for you," he said, in a fierce whisper.

The boy whistled and shrugged his shoulders loose. "You know I ain't goin' to tell tales, grandpa," he said, in a curiously manly fashion.

The old man nodded. "All right, Tommy. I don't believe you be, nuther, but you may jest as well git it through your head what's goin' to happen if you do."

"Ain't goin' to," returned the boy. He whistled charmingly as he raked the leaves. His whistle sounded like the carol of a bird.

Eudora pushed the carriage around to the side door, and immediately there was a fluttering rush of a slender woman clad in lavender down the steps. This woman first kissed Eudora with gentle fervor, then, with a sly look around and voice raised intentionally high, she lifted the blue and white roll from the carriage with the tenderest care. "Did the darling come to see his aunties?" she shrilled.

The old man and the boy in the front yard heard her distinctly. The old man's face was imperturbable. The boy grinned.

Two other women, all clad in lavender, appeared in the doorway. They also bent over the blue and white bundle. They also said something about the darling coming to see his aunties. Then there ensued the softest chorus of lady-laughter, as if at some hidden joke.

"Come in, Eudora dear," said Amelia Lancaster. "Yes, come in, Eudora dear," said Anna Lancaster. "Yes, come in, Eudora dear," said Sophia Willing.

Sophia looked much older than her sisters, but with that exception the resemblance between all three was startling. They always dressed exactly alike, too, in silken fabric of bluish lavender, like myrtle blossoms. Some of the poetical souls in the village called the Lancaster sisters "The ladies in lavender."

There was an astonishing change in the treatment of the blue and white bundle when the sisters and Eudora were in the stately old sitting-room, with its heavy mahogany furniture and its white-wainscoted walls. Amelia simply tossed the bundle into a corner of the sofa; then the sisters all sat in a loving circle around Eudora.

"Are you sure you are not utterly worn out, dear?" asked Amelia, tenderly; and the others repeated the question in exactly the same tone. The Lancaster sisters were not pretty, but all had charming expressions of gentleness and a dignified good-will and loving kindness. Their blue eyes beamed love at Eudora, and it was as if she sat encircled in a soul-ring of affection.

She responded, and her beautiful face glowed with tenderness and pleasure, and something besides, which was as the light of victory.

"I am not in the least tired, thank you, dears," she replied. "Why should I be tired? I am very strong."

Amelia murmured something about such hard work.

"I never thought it would be hard work taking care of a baby," replied Eudora, "and especially such a very light baby."

Something whimsical crept into Eudora's voice; something whimsical crept into the love-light of the other women's eyes. Again a soft ripple of mirth swept over them.

"Especially a baby who never cries," said Amelia.

"No, he never does cry," said Eudora, demurely.

They laughed again. Then Amelia rose and left the room to get the tea-things. The old serving-woman who had lived with them for many years was suffering from rheumatism, and was cared for by her daughter in the little cottage across the road from the Lancaster house. Her husband and grandson were the man and boy at work in the grounds. The three sisters took care of themselves and their house with the elegant ease and lack of fluster of gentlewomen born and bred. Miss Amelia, bringing in the tea-tray, was an unclassed being, neither maid nor mistress, but outranking either. She had tied on a white apron. She bore the silver tray with an ease which bespoke either nerve or muscle in her lace-draped arms.

She poured the tea, holding the silver pot high and letting the amber fluid trickle slowly, and the pearls and diamonds on her thin hands shone dully. Sophia passed little china plates and fringed napkins, and Anna a silver basket with golden squares of sponge-cake.

The ladies ate and drank, and the blue and white bundle on the sofa remained motionless. Eudora, after she had finished her tea, leaned back gracefully in her chair, and her dark eyes gleamed with its mild stimulus. She remained an hour or more. When she went out, Amelia slipped an envelope into her hand and at the same time embraced and kissed her. Sophia and Anna followed her example. Eudora opened her mouth as if to speak, but smiled instead, a fond, proud smile. During the last fifteen minutes of her stay Amelia had slipped out of the room with the blue and white bundle. Now she brought it out and laid it carefully in the carriage.

"We are always so glad to see you, dearest Eudora," said she, "but you understand — "

"Yes," said Sophia, "you understand, Eudora dear, that there is not the slightest haste."

Eudora nodded, and her long neck seemed to grow longer.

When she was stepping regally down the path, Amelia said in a hasty whisper to Sophia: "Did you tell her?"

Sophia shook her head. "No, sister."

"I didn't know but you might have, while I was out of the room."

"I did not," said Sophia. She looked doubtfully at Amelia, then at Anna, and doubt flashed back and forth between the three pairs of blue eyes for a second. Then Sophia spoke with authority, because she was the only one of them all who had entered the estate of matrimony, and had consequently obvious cognizance of such matters.

"I think," said she, "that Eudora should be told that

Harry Lawton has come back and is boarding at the Wellwood Inn."

"You think," faltered Amelia, "that it is possible she might meet him unexpectedly?"

"I certainly do think so. And she might show her feelings in a way which she would ever afterward regret."

"You think, then, that she — "

Sophia gave her sister a look. Amelia fled after Eudora and the baby-carriage. She overtook her at the gate. She laid her hand on Eudora's arm, draped with India shawl.

"Eudora!" she gasped.

Eudora turned her serene face and regarded her questioningly.

"Eudora," said Amelia, "have you heard of anybody's coming to stay at the inn lately?"

"No," replied Eudora, calmly. "Why, dear?"

"Nothing, only, Eudora, a dear and old friend of yours, of ours, is there, so I hear."

Eudora did not inquire who the old friend might be. "Really?" she remarked. Then she said, "Goodby, Amelia dear," and resumed her progress with the baby-carriage.

PART II

"She never even asked who it was," Amelia reported to her sisters, when she had returned to the house. "Because she knew," replied Sophia, sagely; "there has never been any old friend but that one old friend to come back into Eudora Yates's life."

"Has he come back into her life, I wonder?" said Amelia.

"What did he return to Wellwood for if he didn't come for that? All his relatives are gone. He never married. Yes, he has come back to see Eudora and marry her, if she will have him. No man who ever loved Eudora would ever get over loving her. And he will not be shocked when he sees her. She is no more changed than a beautiful old statue."

"*He* is changed, though," said Amelia. "I saw him the other day. He didn't see me, and I would hardly have known him. He has grown stout, and his hair is gray."

"Eudora's hair is gray," said Sophia.

"Yes, but you can see the gold through Eudora's gray. It just looks as if a shadow was thrown over it. It doesn't change her. Harry Lawton's gray hair does change him."

"If," said Anna, sentimentally, "Eudora thinks Harry's hair turned gray for love of her, you can trust her or any woman to see the gold through it."

"Harry's hair was never gold — just an ordinary brown," said Amelia. "Anyway, the Lawtons turned gray young."

"She won't think of that at all," said Sophia.

"I wonder why Eudora always avoided him so, years ago," said Amelia.

"Why doesn't a girl in a field of daisies stop to pick one, which she never forgets?" said Sophia. "Eudora had so many chances, and I don't think her heart was fixed when she was very young; at least, I don't think it was fixed so she knew it."

"I wonder," said Amelia, "if he will go and call on her."

Amelia privately wished that she lived near enough to know if Harry Lawton did call. She, as well as Mrs. Joseph Glynn, would have enjoyed watching out and knowing something of the village happenings, but the Lancaster house was situated so far from the road, behind its grove of trees, that nothing whatever could be seen.

"I doubt if Eudora tells, if he does call — that is, not unless something definite happens," said Anna.

"No," remarked Amelia, sadly. "Eudora is a dear, but she is very silent with regard to her own affairs."

"She ought to be," said Sophia, with her married authority. She was, to her sisters, as one who had passed within the shrine and was dignifiedly silent with regard to its intimate mysteries.

"I suppose so," assented Anna, with a soft sigh.

Amelia sighed also. Then she took the tea-tray out of the room. She had to make some biscuits for supper.

Meantime Eudora was pacing homeward with the baby-carriage. Her serene face was a little perturbed. Her oval cheeks were flushed, and her mouth now and then trembled. She had, if she followed her usual course, to pass the Wellwood Inn, but she could diverge, and by taking a side street and walking a half-mile farther reach home without coming in sight of the inn. She did so today.

When she reached the side street she turned rather swiftly and gave a little sigh of relief. She was afraid that she might meet Harry Lawton. It was a lonely way. There was a brook on one side, bordered thickly with bushy willows which were turning gold-green. On the other side were undulating pasture-lands on which grazed a few sheep. There were no houses until she reached the turn which would lead back to the main street, on which her home was located.

Eudora was about midway of this street when she saw a man approaching. He was a large man clad in gray, and he was swinging an umbrella. Somehow the swing of that umbrella, even from a distance, gave an impression of embarrassment and boyish hesitation. Eudora did not know him at first. She had expected to see the same Harry Lawton who had gone away. She did not expect to see a stout, middle-aged man, but a slim youth.

However, as they drew nearer each other, she knew; and curiously enough it was that swing of the tightly furled umbrella which gave her the clue. She knew Harry because of that. It was a little boyish trick which had survived time. It was too late for her to draw back, for he had seen her, and Eudora was keenly alive to the indignity of abruptly turning and scuttling away with the tail of her black silk swishing, her India shawl trailing, and the baby-carriage bumping over the furrows. She continued, and Harry Lawton continued, and they met.

Harry Lawton had known Eudora at once. She looked the same to him as when she had been a girl, and he looked the same to her when he spoke.

"Hullo, Eudora," said Harry Lawton, in a ludicrously boyish fashion. His face flushed, too, like a boy. He extended his hand like a boy. The man, seen near at hand, was a boy. In reality he himself had not changed. A few layers of flesh and a change of color-cells do not make another man. He had always been a simple, sincere, friendly soul, beloved of men and women alike, and he was that now. Eudora held out her hand, and her eyes fell before the eyes of the man, in an absurd fashion for such a stately creature as she. But the man himself acted like a great happy overgrown school-boy.

"Hullo, Eudora," he said again.

"Hullo," said she, falteringly.

It was inconceivable that they should meet in such wise after the years of separation and longing which they had both undergone; but each took refuge, as it were, in a long-past youth, even childhood, from the fierce tension of age. When they were both children they had been accustomed to pass each other on the village street with exactly such salutation, and now both reverted to it. The tall, regal woman in her India shawl and the stout, middle-aged man had both stepped back to their vantage-ground of springtime to meet.

However, after a moment, Eudora reasserted herself. "I only heard a short time ago that you were here," she said, in her usual even voice. The fair oval of her face was as serene and proud toward the man as the face of the moon.

The man swung his umbrella, then began prodding the ground with it. "Hullo, Eudora," he said again; then he added: "How are you, anyway? Fine and well?"

"I am very well, thank you," said Eudora. "So you have come home to Wellwood after all this time?"

The man made an effort and recovered himself, although his handsome face was burning.

"Yes," he remarked, with considerable ease and dignity, to which he had a right, for Harry Lawton had not made a failure of his life, even though it had not included Eudora and a fulfilled dream.

"Yes," he continued, "I had some leisure; in fact, I have this spring retired from business; and I thought I would have a look at the old place. Very little changed I am happy to find it."

"Yes, it is very little changed," assented Eudora; "at least, it seems so to me, but it is not for a life-long dweller in any place to judge of change. It is for the one who goes and returns after many years."

There was a faint hint of proud sadness in Eudora's

voice as she spoke the last two words.

"It has been many years," said Lawton, gravely, "and I wonder if it has seemed so to you."

Eudora held her head proudly. "Time passes swiftly," said she, tritely.

"But sometimes it may seem long in the passing, however swift," said Lawton, "though I suppose it has not to you. You look just the same," he added, regarding her admiringly.

Eudora flushed a little. "I must be changed," she murmured.

"Not a bit. I would have known you anywhere. But I — "

"I knew you the minute you spoke."

"Did you?" he asked, eagerly. "I was afraid I had grown so stout you would not remember me at all. Queer how a man will grow stout. I am not such a big eater, either, and I have worked hard, and — well, I might have been worse off, but I must say I have seen men who seemed to me happier, though I have made the best of things. I always did despise a flunk. But you! I heard you had adopted a baby," he said, with a sudden glance at the blue and white bundle in the carriage, "and I thought you were mighty sensible. When people grow old they want young people growing around them, staffs for old age, you know, and all that sort of thing. Don't know but I should have adopted a boy myself if it hadn't been for — "

The man stopped, and his face was pink. Eudora turned her face slightly away.

"By the way," said the man, in a suddenly hushed voice, "I suppose the kid you've got there is asleep. Wouldn't do to wake him?"

"I think I had better not," replied Eudora, in a hesitating voice. She began to walk along, and Harry Lawton fell into step beside her.

"I suppose it isn't best to wake up babies; makes them cross, and they cry," he said. "Say, Eudora, is he much trouble?"

"Very little," replied Eudora, still in that strange voice.

"Doesn't keep you awake nights?"

"Oh no."

"Because if he does, I really think you should have a nurse. I don't think you ought to lose sleep taking care of him."

"I do not."

"Well, I was mighty glad when I heard you had adopted him. I suppose you made sure about his parentage, where he hailed from and what sort of people?"

"Oh yes." Eudora was very pale.

"That's right. Maybe some time you will tell me all about it. I am coming over Thursday to have a look at the youngster. I have to go to the city on business tomorrow and can't get back until Thursday. I was coming over tonight to call on you, but I have a man coming to the inn this evening — he called me up on the telephone just now — one of the men who have taken my place in the business; and as long as I have met you I will just walk along with you, and come Thursday. I suppose the baby won't be likely to wake up just yet, and when he does you'll have to get his supper and put him to bed. Is that the way the rule goes?"

Eudora nodded in a shamed, speechless sort of way.

"All right. I'll come Thursday -but say, look here, Eudora. This is a quiet road, not a soul in sight, just like an outdoor room to ourselves. Why shouldn't I know now just as well as wait? Say, Eudora, you know how I used to feel about you. Well, it has lasted all these years. There has never been another woman I even cared to look at. You are alone, except for that baby, and I am alone. Eudora — "

The man hesitated. His flushed face had paled. Eudora paced silently and waveringly at his side.

"Eudora," the man went on, "you know you always used to run away from me — never gave me a chance to really ask; and I thought you didn't care. But somehow I have wondered — perhaps because you never got married — if you didn't quite mean it, if you didn't quite know your own mind. You'll think I'm a conceited ass, but I'm not a bad sort, Eudora. I would be as good to you as I know how, and — we could bring him up together." He pointed to the carriage. "I have plenty of money. We could do anything we wanted to do for him, and we should not have to live alone. Say, Eudora, you may not think it's the thing for a man to own up to, but, hang it all! I'm alone, and I don't want to face the rest of my life alone. Eudora, do you think you could make up your mind to marry me, after all?"

They had reached the turn in the road. Just beyond

rose the stately pile of the old Yates mansion. Eudora stood still and gave one desperate look at her lover. "I will let you know Thursday," she gasped. Then she was gone, trundling the baby- carriage with incredible speed.

"But, Eudora — "

"I must go," she called back, faintly. The man stood staring after the hurrying figure with its swishing black skirts and its flying points of rich India shawl, and he smiled happily and tenderly. That evening at the inn his caller, a young fellow just married and beaming with happiness, saw an answering beam in the older man's face. He broke off in the midst of a sentence and stared at him.

"Don't give me away until I tell you to, Ned," he said, "but I don't know but I am going to follow your example."

"My example?"

"Yes, going to get married."

The young man gasped. A look of surprise, of amusement, then of generous sympathy came over his face. He grasped Lawton's hand.

"Who is she?"

"Oh, a woman I wanted more than anything in the world when I was about your age."

"Then she isn't young?"

"She is better than young."

"Well," agreed the young man, "being young and pretty is not everything."

"Pretty!" said Harry Lawton, scornfully, "pretty!

She is a great beauty."

"And not young?"

"She is a great beauty, and better than young, because time has not touched her beauty, and you can see for yourself that it lasts."

The young man laughed. "Oh, well," he said, with a tender inflection, "I dare say that my Amy will look like that to me."

"If she doesn't you don't love her," said Lawton. "But my Eudora *is* that."

"That is a queer-sounding Greek name."

"She is Greek, like her name. Such beauty never grows old. She stands on her pedestal, and time only looks at her to love her."

"I thought you were a business man as hard as nails," said the young man, wonderingly. Lawton laughed.

When Thursday came, Lawton, carefully dressed and carrying a long tissue-paper package, evidently of roses, approached the Yates house. It was late in the afternoon. There had been a warm day, and the trees were clouds of green and more bushes had blossomed. Eudora had put on a green silk dress of her youth. The revolving fashions had made it very passable, and the fabric was as beautiful as ever.

When Lawton presented her with the roses she pinned one in the yellowed lace which draped her bodice and put the rest in a great china vase on the table. The roses were very fragrant, and immediately the whole room was possessed by them.

A tiny, insistent cry came from a corner, and Lawton and Eudora turned toward it. There stood the old wooden cradle in which Eudora had been rocked to sleep, but over the clumsy hood Eudora had tacked a fall of rich old lace and a great bow of soft pink satin.

"He is waking up," said the man, in a hushed, almost reverent voice.

Eudora nodded. She went toward the cradle, and the man followed. She lifted the curtain of lace, and there became visible little feebly waving pink arms and hands, like tentacles of love, and a little puckered pink face which was at once ugly and divinely beautiful.

"A fine boy," said the man. The baby made a grimace at him which was hideous but lovely.

"I do believe he thinks he knows you," said Eudora, foolishly.

The baby made a little nestling motion, and its creasy eyelids dropped.

"Looks to me as if he was going to sleep again," said Lawton, in a whisper. Eudora jogged the cradle gently with her foot, and both were still. Then Eudora dropped the lace veil over the cradle again and moved softly away.

Lawton followed her. "I haven't my answer yet, Eudora," he whispered, leaning over her shoulder as she moved.

"Come into the other room," she murmured, "or we shall wake the baby." Her voice was softly excited.

Eudora led the way into the parlor, upon whose walls hung some really good portraits and whose furnishings still merited the adjective magnificent. There had been opulence in the Yates family; and in this room, which had been conserved, there was still undimmed and unfaded evidence of it. Eudora drew aside a brocade curtain and sat down on an embroidered satin sofa. Lawton sat beside her.

"This room looks every whit as grand as it used to look to me when I was a boy," he said.

"It has hardly been opened, except to have it cleaned, since you went away," replied Eudora, "and no wear has come upon it."

"And everything was rather splendid to begin with, and has lasted. And so were you, Eudora, and you have lasted. Well, what about my answer, dear girl?"

"You have to hear something first."

Lawton laughed. "A confession?"

Eudora held her head proudly. "No, not exactly," said she. "I am not sure that I have ever had anything to confess."

"You never were sure, you proud creature."

"I am not now. I never intended to deceive you, but you were deceived. I did intend to deceive others, others who had no right to know. I do not feel that I owe them any explanation. I do owe you one, although I do not feel that I have done anything wrong. Still, I cannot allow you to remain deceived."

"Well, what is it, dear?"

Eudora looked at him. "You remember that afternoon when you met me with the baby-carriage?"

"Well, I should think so. My memory has not failed me in three days."

"You thought I had a baby in that carriage."

"Of course I did."

"There wasn't a baby in the carriage."

"Well, what on earth was it, then? A cat?"

Eudora, if possible, looked prouder. "It was a package of soiled linen from the Lancaster girls."

"Oh, good heavens, Eudora!"

"Yes," said Eudora, proudly. "I lost nearly everything when that railroad failed. I had enough left to pay the taxes, and that was all. After I had used a small sum in the savings-bank there was nothing. One day I went over to the Lancasters', and I — well, I had not had much to eat for several days. I was a little faint, and — "

"Eudora, you poor, darling girl!"

"And the Lancaster girls found out," continued Eudora, calmly. "They gave me something to eat, and I suppose I ate as if I were famished. I was."

"Eudora!"

"And they wanted to give me money, but I would not take it, and they had been trying to find a laundress for their finer linen — their old serving-woman was ill. They could find one for the heavier things, but they are very particular, and I was sure I could manage, and so I begged them to let me have the work, and they did, and overpaid me, I fear. And I — I knew very well how many spying eyes were about, and I thought of my proud father and my proud mother and grandmother, and perhaps I was proud, too. You know they talk about the Yates pride. It was not so much because I was ashamed of doing honest work as because I did resent those prying eyes and tattling tongues, and so I said nothing, but I did go back and forth in broad daylight with the linen wrapped up in the old blue and white blanket, in my old carriage, and they thought what they thought."

Eudora laughed faintly. She had a gentle humor. "It was somewhat laughable, too," she observed. "The Lancaster girls and I have had our little jests over it, but I felt that I could not deceive you."

Lawton looked bewildered. "But that is a real baby in there," he said, jerking an elbow toward the other room.

"Oh yes," replied Eudora. "I adopted him yesterday. I went to the Children's Home in Elmfield. Amelia Lancaster went with me. Wilson drove us over. I know a nurse there. She took care of mother in her last illness. And I adopted this baby; at least, I am going to. He comes of respectable people, and his parents are dead. His mother died when he was born. He is healthy, and I thought him a beautiful baby."

"Yes, he is," assented Lawton, but he still looked somewhat perplexed. "But why did you hurry off so and get him, Eudora?" said he.

"I thought from what you said that day that you would be disappointed when you found out I had only the Lancaster linen and not a real baby," said Eudora with her calm, grand air and with no trace of a smile.

"Then that means that you say yes, Eudora?"

For the first time Eudora gave a startled glance at him. "Didn't you know?" she gasped.

"How should I? You had not said yes really, dear."

"Do you think," said Eudora Yates, "that I am not too proud to allow you to ask me if my answer were not yes?"

"So that is the reason you always ran away from me, years ago, so that I never had a chance to ask you?"

"Of course," said Eudora. "No woman of my family ever allows a declaration which she does not intend to accept. I was always taught that by my mother."

Then a small but insistent cry rent the air. "The baby is awake!" cried Eudora, and ran, or, rather, paced swiftly — Eudora had been taught never to run — and Lawton followed. It was he who finally quieted the child, holding the little thing in his arms.

But the baby, before that, cried so long and lustily that all the women in the Glynn house opposite were on the alert, and also some of the friends who were calling there. Abby Simson was one.

"Harry Lawton has been there over an hour now," said Abby, while the wailing continued, "and I know as well as I want to that there will be a wedding."

"I wonder he doesn't object to that adopted baby," said Julia Esterbrook.

"I know one thing," said Abby Simson. "It must be a boy baby, it hollers so."

THE END